The Paci Fairy

Created and Written by

Melissa Burnett

Illustrated by

Chrisann Zaubi

Dedication

To my Father, Gene:
For believing in me – you are my Hero.

To my Mother, Micki and Stepfather, John:
For your unconditional love and support.

To my Brother, Darin:
For your vision and strength.

To my Soul Sister, Amy Jo:
For always being there and helping me to stay aligned with my true spirit.

To my Husband, Brock:
My love, my life.
For your tenacity, patience and creativity - you are the moment that takes my breath away.

To my daughter, Alexis:
My heart and my inspiration.

There once was a little village,
a nice place known as Pacitown,
where the people could use their mouths
to talk and laugh and smile and frown.

Pacies are only for babies,
to help them sleep tight through the night,
to help them when teething
and make them feel safe and alright.

When a baby grows older
and becomes a big girl or boy,
that's when the Paci Fairy comes
and trades their Paci for a toy.

After The Paci Fairy comes
and takes your Paci for a toy,
she gives your Paci to new parents
for their new babies to enjoy.

Pacitown was full of laughter
in the rain, the sun, or the snow.
Until one strange and rainy night,
The Paci Fairy did not show.

The small town was in great danger,
as anyone could have told her,
because the Pacies stayed in mouths,
Even as people got older.

No one could talk with their Pacies.
The teacher could not speak or teach.
Everyone was mumbling.
Even the preacher could not preach.

When people got sick or felt ill,
the village doctor could not say
just what medicine they should take
with his old Paci in the way.

Everyone in Pacitown,
from the old down to the young,
could not express how they felt,
because the Paci had their tongue.

The townspeople were very sad.
No one was hugging and kissing.
Their old Pacies were in the way
and it was love, they were missing.

All of the children stood and stared.
They couldn't say each others' names.
Pacitown playground was empty
because they couldn't play their games.

All the new babies started to cry
and the parents started to weep.
There were no Pacies left to give
to the babies who could not sleep.

Pacitown was in big trouble,
the small village in a whirl.
Only one person could save them,
she was a brave little girl.

Everyone called her Palina,
as in "Palina Paciloo".
This adventurous young lady
thought she knew just what to do!

She filled her backpack with supplies
and finished doing her last chore.
To go find the Paci Fairy,
she boldly headed out the door.

She walked through giant green forests
and splashed across sparkling streams.
She danced under gorgeous rainbows
and chased after yellow sunbeams.

She hiked over hills and mountains
and jumped over piles of sticks.
She skipped down trails and through meadows
and climbed over slippery bricks.

Palina was lost and tired.
She sat on a long narrow bridge
and saw a tiny little home
sitting alone up on a ridge.

The house had a red picket fence,
purple flowers in full bloom,
bright orange thatching on the roof,
and on the porch a swing and broom.

As she approached the pink mailbox,
which clearly read "The Paci Fairy"
Palina thought how magical.
It is quite extraordinary!

Her blue eyes sparkled, she smiled,
and then with glee jumped up and down.
She had found The Paci Fairy,
who alone could save Pacitown.

The
Paci
Fairy

She pushed through the purple flowers
because the long pathway was blocked.
She finally reached the big red door,
and then...she bravely knocked.

An old lady wearing a shawl,
with gray hair down to the floor
and the sweetest eyes ever seen,
opened up the cottage door.

"Yes?" she asked with a lovely smile.
"Can I help you out, my dear?"
She had no Paci in her mouth
and her words were very clear.

Palina tried to speak to her.
The lady waved her hand,
"Here, let me take your Paci, dear,
I cannot understand."

"Thank you Ma'am. Now I can talk!
And I have reached my goal at last!
Have you seen The Paci Fairy?
Pacitown needs her magic fast."

"Come on inside" the lady spoke,
with a slight twinkle in her eyes.
"I am sitting here before you.
Please forgive my old disguise."

The Paci Fairy smiled sweetly,
"Until you came, things seemed quite bleak.
After working hard for many years,
I have grown old and very weak."

"I just knew that someone special
would come along and take my place.
Someone helpful I can work with,
someone brave, who will embrace...

the magic of being a Fairy–
a person with a great big heart,
someone who loves all the children,
who is dear and also smart."

"I don't get it," said Palina,
"you are looking for someone new?"
"That's right," said The Paci Fairy,
" and that special someone is YOU!"

"I will train you fully," she said
to Palina's gleaming face.
"When you have learned all I can teach,
you will be free to take my place."

Palina agreed right away,
she didn't even have to think.
When The Fairy waved her wand,
Palina's hair grew long and pink!

She learned how to open windows,
tiptoe quiet through the night.
She learned how to collect Pacies,
and stay safely out of sight.

The Fairy then taught Palina
how to use the stars in the sky.
They flew together holding hands
and then Palina learned to fly.

They flew to Pacitown that night
and searched each house and door.
They gathered all the Pacies
that were not needed anymore.

The next Morning all the people
talked 'til their faces turned blue!
They were asking one another,
"What's your name?" and "How are you?"

All the students were now learning,
because the teachers could now teach.
All the people were now praying because
the preachers could now preach.

Children were laughing and singing
because they knew what they were saying.
Pacitown playground was now full
and all of the kids were playing.

The Pacies had been restored!
Babies were sleeping, not whining.
Pacitown came back to life
with music, dancing, and dining.

All the mommies and the daddies
were now hugging and kissing.
Pacitown was back to normal
with their old Pacies missing.

As the many years went by,
Palina worked night and day,
giving toys to every child,
who gave their Paci away.

One day, the nice lady told her,
"I'm giving you my Fairy things.
You are now The Paci Fairy
and you have really earned your wings!

You've learned everything I know
and of you I have grown quite fond.
I would be very honored, dear,
to give to you my crown and wand."

Palina was filled with delight,
as she wore her new Fairy crown,
which you can see in the moonlight
as she flies at night through your town.

So, kids, when you are ready,
to become a big girl or boy,
ask Palina to fly over
and trade your Paci for a toy!